A CAITLYN DLOUHY BOOK

Atheneum   NEW YORK   LONDON   TORONTO   SYDNEY   NEW DELHI

JASON REYNOLDS

LONG WAY DOWN

THE GRAPHIC NOVEL

WITH ART BY
DANICA NOVGORODOFF

atheneum

An imprint of Simon & Schuster Children's Publishing Division
1230 Avenue of the Americas, New York, New York 10020

Text © 2017 by Jason Reynolds
Cover illustration © 2020 by Danica Novgorodoff
Cover design by Sonia Chaghatzbanian © 2020 by Simon & Schuster, Inc.
Interior illustration © 2020 by Danica Novgorodoff
Adapted from Long Way Down by Jason Reynolds, published by Atheneum in 2017

For information about special discounts for bulk purchases, please contact Simon & Schuster
Special Sales at 1-866-506-1949 or business@simonandschuster.com.
The Simon & Schuster Speakers Bureau can bring authors to your live event. For more information
or to book an event, contact the Simon & Schuster Speakers Bureau at 1-866-248-3049 or visit
our website at www.simonspeakers.com.
Also available in an Atheneum hardcover edition
Interior design by Sonia Chaghatzbanian
The text for this book was set in Danica Novgorodoff.
The illustrations for this book were rendered in ink and watercolor.
Manufactured in China
First Atheneum paperback edition February 2022
10 9 8 7 6 5 4 3 2
The Library of Congress has cataloged the hardcover edition as follows:
Names: Reynolds, Jason, author. | Novgorodoff, Danica, illustrator.
Title: Long way down : the graphic novel / Jason Reynolds ; illustrated by Danica Novgorodoff.
Description: New York : Atheneum, [2020] | Audience: Ages 14 up. | Audience: Grades 10–12. |
Summary: As Will, fifteen, sets out to avenge his brother Shawn's fatal shooting, seven ghosts
who knew Shawn board the elevator and reveal truths Will needs to know.
Identifiers: LCCN 2020012981 (print) | LCCN 2020012982 (eBook) | ISBN 9781534444959
(hardcover) | ISBN 9781534444966 (pbk) | ISBN 9781534444973 (eBook)
Subjects: LCSH: Graphic novels. | CYAC: Graphic novels. | Murder—Fiction. | Revenge—Fiction. |
Ghosts—Fiction. | Brothers—Fiction. | Conduct of life—Fiction.
Classification: LCC PZ7.7.R4915 Lon 2020 (print) | LCC PZ7.7.R4915 (eBook) | DDC 741.5/973—dc23
LC record available at https://lccn.loc.gov/2020012981
LC eBook record available at https://lccn.loc.gov/2020012982
0822 SCP

For all the young
brothers and sisters in
detention centers around
the country, the ones
I've seen, and the ones I
haven't. You are loved.
—J. R.

To the young artists,
writers, and activists
working for justice.
Tell your stories.
—D. N.

LONG

WAY

DOWN

Don't nobody believe
nothing these days,

which is why I haven't
told nobody the story
I'm about to tell you.

You probably ain't gon' believe it either,
gon' think I'm lying
or I'm losing it,
but I'm telling you...

My name is Will.
William.
William Holloman.

But to my friends
and people
who *know me*
know me,

just Will.

I'm only William
to my mother

and my brother, Shawn,
whenever he was trying
to be funny.

Y'all are what, fifteen? I grew a foot when I was fifteen.

Like a foot and a half. I got all his old shirts he couldn't fit.

Even though Tony was the best ballplayer around here our age, he was also the shortest.

And everybody knows you can't go all the way when you're that small

unless you can really jump.

Like...

Everybody
ran,
ducked,
hid,
tucked
themselves tight.

Did what we've all
been trained to do.

Me and Tony
waited like we always do,

Pressed our lips to the
pavement and prayed
the boom, followed by
the buzz of a bullet,

for the rumble to stop,

ain't meet us.

Shawn.

I've never been

in an earthquake.

Don't know if this was

even close to how they

are, but the ground

defi nitely felt like

it o pened up

and ate me.

I don't know you,
don't know
your last name,

if you got
brothers
or sisters
or mothers
or fathers
or cousins
        that be like

brothers
and sisters
or aunties
or uncles
        that be like

mothers
and fathers,

Or maybe somehow

join him.

In that bag,
    special soap
        for my mother's eczema.

I've seen her scratch until it bleeds.

Curse the invisible thing trying to eat her.

Maybe there's something invisible
    trying to eat
        all of us as
            if we are beef.

When bad things happen,
we can usually look up and see
the moon, big and bright,
shining over us.

But when Shawn
died,
the moon was off.

Somebody told me once a month
the moon blacks out
and becomes new.

I'll tell you one thing,

the moon is lucky it's not down here

where nothing

is ever

new.

The Rules

No.1: Crying

Don't.
No matter what.
Don't.

No.2: Snitching

Don't.
No matter what.
Don't.

No.3: RevenGe

If someone you love
gets killed,

find the person
who killed
them and...

I won't pretend that Shawn
was the kind of guy
who was home before curfew.

After he turned eighteen,
our mother used to tell him,

It

used

to be

different.

When I was twelve and he
was sixteen, we would talk
till one of us passed out.

He would tell me about
girls, and I would
tell him about pretend girls,

TUPAC

who he pretended were real, too,
just to make me feel good.

He would tell me stories about
how the best rappers were
Biggie and Tupac,

but I always wondered if that was
just because they were dead.

People always
love people more
when they're dead.

I'll never go to sleep again
believing Shawn will eventually come home
because he won't

and now I guess
I should love him more,
like he's my favorite,

which is hard to do
because he was my only
brother, and

already my favorite.

A cannon
A strap
A piece
A biscuit
A burner

.45 Auto

A heater
A chopper
A gat
A hammer
A tool

For RULE No. 3.

Which brings me to Carlson Riggs.

He was known around here for being as loud as police sirens but as soft as his first name.

People said Riggs talked so much trash because he was short, but I think it was because his mom made him take gymnastics when he was a kid, and when you wear tights and know how to do cartwheels it might be a good idea to also know how to defend yourself.

Or at least talk like you can.

Riggs and Shawn were so-called friends.

To land on your feet, you gotta time it just right.

Shawn taught me how to time it perfectly.

was shoot him.

No. 1:
TURF

abandoned
parking lot

JR playground

P.S. 92

Riggs moved to a
different part of the hood
where the Dark Suns
hang and bang and be wild.

SuperLaundry

bus stop

our building

Tony's Pizza

He wanted to join so he
could have a backbone built for him
by the bite of his block boys
who wait for anyone to cross
the line into their territory,

Library

OJ's Fruit
Market

which happens to be nine
blocks from our building,
and in the same
neighborhood
as the corner store

corner store

DARK SUNS

do not cross

Baptist
Church

Catholic
Church

that sells that special soap
my mother sent Shawn
out to get for her the
day before yesterday.

Elli's Deli

Thrifty
Pharmacy

Abels Car Wash

Caribbean
Bakery

Valu Foods

Top Cutz

Get

body

down

some

with

by

some

down

body

beat

or

get

No.2: CRIME SHOWS

I grew up watching crime shows with my mother.

Always knew who the killer was way before the cops.

It's like a gift,
solving murder cases.

Had to be.

I had never held a gun.

5:32:55 a.m.

EXPRESS
ACY Inc.

I wrapped my fingers
around the grip, placing
them over Shawn's

like little
brother holding big
brother's hand again,

8:41:16 a.m.

walking me to the store,
teaching me how to
do a Penny Drop.

If you let go too early
you'll land on your face.

If you let go too
late you'll land
on your back.

To land on your feet,
you gotta time it just right.

The plan
was

to wait for Riggs in front of his building.

Me and Shawn were always over his house before Riggs joined the gang,

and since then, Shawn had been up that way a bunch of times to get Mom's special soap.

NO SMOKING

CAPACITY 2000 LBS

CITY ID NO. 3P577Q

Couldn't be.

Couldn't be.

Buck?

Ain't that
what it say?

Couldn't be.

Couldn't be.

But I thought...

I thought...
I thought...

You thought I
was dead.

I rubbed my eyes

over and

over and

over and

over again,

trippin'.

Never smoked
or nothing like that.

Don't know high life.
Don't know bad trips.

Don't no dead man supposed to be talking to me, though.

Yeah, I did.

I was hoping he would come back with I'm not dead or I faked my death or

something like that.

Or maybe I'd wake up, sit straight up in bed, the gun still tucked under my pillow, my mother still asleep at the kitchen table.

A dream.

I am.

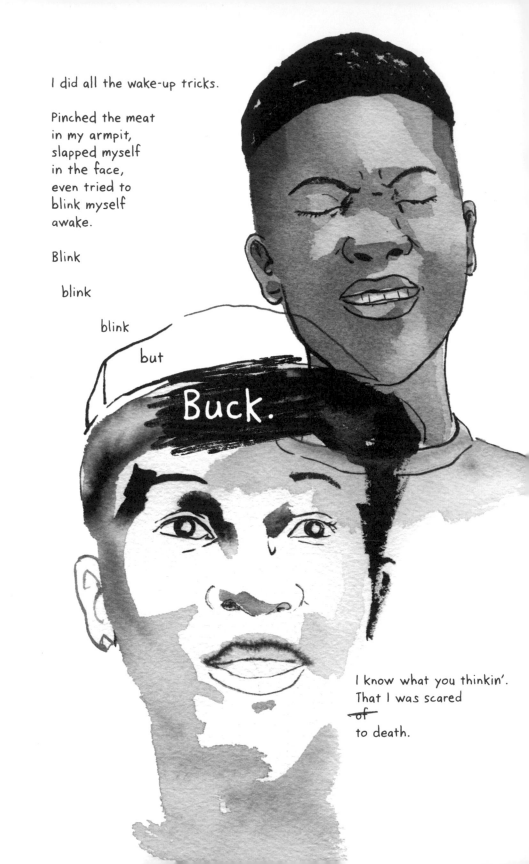

But no need to be afraid.
I had known Buck
since I was a kid
the only big brother
Shawn had ever had.

Shawn knew Buck
better than I did,
knew Buck longer than
we'd known our dad.

I take it back.
I *was* scared.
What if he had come
    to take me with him?

What if he had come
to catch
my breath?

So why you
here?

NO SMOKING

CAPACITY 2000 LBS

CITY ID NO. 3P577Q

I thought he was
only my ghost,

my imagination.

But when she could see him,
smell his funky cigarette,
I knew for a fact
this was real.

I didn't know
guns were allowed
in elevators either.

His cig
was burning

but not burning down.

Smoke. But no ash.

I swear sometimes
it feels like God

be flashing photos
of his children,

awkward,
amazing,

tucked into his wallet
for the world
to see.

But the world
    don't wanna see
    no kids,

and God ain't
no pushy parent

so he just folds
    and snaps

us shut.

Dani was killed
before she ever learned
The Rules.

So I explained them to
her so she wouldn't think
less of me for following
them

like I was just another
block boy on one
looking to off one.

So that she knew I had
purpose

and that this was about
family

and had I known
The Rules when we
were kids I would've
done the same thing

for her.

What

if

you

miss?

NO SMOKING

CAPACITY 2000 LBS

CITY ID NO. 3P577Q

Thought when the
doors opened the
smoke would rush out.

But instead it
became a still cloud
trapped in a steel cube.

Smoke   like spirit
can be thick but
ain't supposed to be
nothing solid
enough to hold me.

I expected whoever
was waiting to wait
for the next one.

Who wants to get
on an elevator
full of smoke?

Koff
Koff

There are
so many pictures
of Uncle Mark in
our house.

Posing with my father, his shorter
younger brother.

Camera ready.

Fly.

Like Shawn.

Foreshadowing the flash.

Story No.1

ABOUT UNCLE MARK

He videotaped everything with a camera his mother, my grandmother, bought him

for his eighteenth birthday.

But he dreamed of making a movie.

Script idea:

BOY: Mickey. No game.
No girls. Meets
GIRL: Jesse, the young
girlfriend of
BOY: Mickey's landlord.
GIRL: Jesse teaches
BOY: Mickey everything he
needs to know about
GIRL: How to impress them.
How to treat them. But
BOY: Mickey uses what he
learns to get
GIRL: Jesse to fall in love with
him, but her boyfriend,
BOY: Mickey's landlord, finds
out and kicks him and
GIRL: Jesse out of the building.
So they're in love,
but they're homeless,
but they're happy.

Riiiight.

CASTING OF THE WORST, STUPIDEST MOVIE EVER:

BOY: Mickey
to be played by Uncle Mark's little brother, my father, Mikey.

GIRL: Jesse
to be played by the younger sister of a girl
Uncle Mark used to date, Shari, my mother.

Story No.2
ABOUT UNCLE MARK

Uncle Mark lost the camera his mother got him. Couldn't afford another one.

Options:

Could've asked Grandma again, but that would've been pointless. Could've stolen one, but he wasn't 'bout to be sweating, so he wasn't 'bout to be running.

Could've gotten a job, but working was another one of those things Uncle Mark just wasn't 'bout to be doing.
So he did what a lot of people do around here.

Uncle Mark was
a full-out pusher,
money-making
pretty boy,

target
for a ruthless
young hustler
whose name
Mom can never
remember.

BOAR HEAD PRODUCTS
oli's GROCERY

BAM

3.5

That guy took the corner
from Uncle Mark.
Everybody ran ducked hid tucked
blew their own eardrums
gouged their own eyes.

Did what they'd all
been trained to do.

Uncle Mark should've
just bought his camera
and shot his stupid movie
after the first day.

Unfortunately,
he never shot nothing
ever again.

But my father did.

NO SMOKING

CAPACITY 2000 LBS

CITY ID NO. 3P577Q

There he was.
Recognized him instantly.

Been waiting
for him since
I was three.

I have no memories of my father.

Shawn always tried to get me to remember things like

Pop dressing up as Michael Jackson for Halloween, and, after trick-or-treating,

riding us up and down
on this elevator,
doing his best
moonwalk.

Shawn swore I laughed
so hard I farted.

I was only three.
And I don't
remember that.

A broken heart
killed my dad.
That's what my mother
always said.

As a kid
I always figured
his heart
was forreal broken

like an arm
or a toy
or Shawn's middle dresser drawer.

But that's not what Shawn said.

Shawn always said
our dad was killed
for killing the man
who killed our uncle.

Said he was at a pay
phone, probably talking
to Mom, when a guy
walked up on him,

put a pistol to his head,
asked him if he knew a
guy who went by Gee.
Don't know what Pop said.

But that was the end
of that story.

09:08:32 a.m.

But I don't remember none of that, either.

Hi, Will.

My father's voice brand-new to me.

I don't know,
I don't know—

what to do.

No crying.

Not in front of Pop.

Not in front of
no one.

Never.

What you
think you
should do?

Follow
The Rules.
Just like you
did.

You ever heard
your father's
story, Will?

Of course.

That *something*
must be

what my mom

meant by

the nighttime.

My father was not
like I had imagined him.

Spent my whole damn life
missing a misser.

Wasn't sure what *he* was thinking.

Maybe that I was exactly how *he* had imagined.

Maybe that disappointed him.

You would think
I would be thinking
about whether or not
he could actually do it

since he wasn't real.

But the hugs were real.
And the gun was real.

Weren't no ghost bullets
in that clip.

Those were real bullets.

Fifteen total.
One for every year
of my life.

NO SMOKING

CAPACITY 2000 LBS

CITY ID NO. 3P577Q

9   10   11

6   7   8

3   4   5

B   L   2

09:08:47 a.m.

A stranger

a normal guy.

Didn't acknowledge nobody.

No dead body.
No live body.
No smoke.

Normal.

but
made me real

happy
I wasn't all

the way gone.

Buck's real name
was James.

Buck short
for young-buck.
Nickname given
by stepfather as a joke
because Buck
couldn't grow no facial hair.

Smooth baby face.

Buck was two-sided.
Two dads, step and real.

Step raised him:
a preacher, not scared of no one,
praying for anyone, helping everyone.

Real run through him:
a bank robber,
would steal air from the world
if he could get his hands on it.

People always said
he was taught to do good
but doing bad
was in his blood.

And there's that nighttime
  Mom always be talking about.

    It'll snatch your teaching
    from you,
      put a gun in your hand,
      a grumble in your gut,
      and some sharp in your teeth.

But he didn't start that way.
At first Buck was
a small-time hustler,
dime bags on the corner.

Same old story
until my pop got popped
and Buck became a big brother
to Shawn

and a robber to a bunch of
suburban neighborhoods

and come back with
money (the most)
sneakers (the best)
and jewelry (the finest).

That was the one time I heard Buck's real name.

Shawn ain't say nothing to the cops, to no one, just locked himself in his room for hours.

No. 1: TurF

nine blocks from
where I live.

No. 2: The ShiNing

a cigarette burn
under the right eye.

No. 3:
DARK DeeD

robbing someone,
beating someone,
or the worst,

Tony talking
ain't the same as snitching.
Snitching is bumping gums
to badges, but Tony talking
was laying claim,
loyalty,

an allegiance to
the asphalt around
here, an attempt
to grow taller
get bigger
one way or another.

NO SMOKING

CAPACITY 2000 LBS

CITY ID NO. 3P577Q

When we were kids
I would follow Shawn
around the apartment
making the strangest
noise with my mouth.

Like a burp mixed
with a yawn mixed
with hum.

For twenty
minutes straight.

To punish me,
he would wait for me
to run out of steam

and then, to my surprise,
he wouldn't say a word to me
for the rest
of the day.

NO SMOKING

CAPACITY 2000 LBS

CITY ID NO. 3P577Q

09:09:09 a.m.

Also by Jason Reynolds

When I Was the Greatest

The Boy in the Black Suit

All American Boys

As Brave As You

Long Way Down

For Every One

Look Both Ways

The Track Series:

Ghost

Patina

Sunny

Lu

JASON REYNOLDS has won a bunch of awards, and been a bunch of places, and met a bunch of young people and older people who love young people. So, Jason Reynolds . . . needs a nap. But how can he rest, when there're still so many places to go? How can he rest, when stories like this one—of loss, and fear, and anger—are still so common in real life, and not nearly as beautiful as the art in this book? How can he rest (tell me, how?), when he still hasn't met you? Visit Jason at jasonwritesbooks.com.

DANICA NOVGORODOFF loves to draw, paint, play soccer, eat ice cream, read stories, write stories, and adapt great stories like this one into graphic novels. She's from Brooklyn, NY, and Louisville, KY. This is her fifth graphic novel. Find Danica at danicanovgorodoff.com.